Lucky Leaf

KEVIN O'MALLEY

WALKER & COMPANY

NEW YORK

First published in the United States of America in 2004 by Walker Publishing Company, Inc.
Paperback edition published in 2007

For information about permission to reproduce selections from this book,
write to Permissions, Walker & Company, 175 Fifth Avenue, New York, New York 10010

The Library of Congress has cataloged the hardcover edition as follows:
O'Malley, Kevin.
Lucky leaf / Kevin O'Malley.
p.   cm.
Summary: After his mother tells him to stop playing video games and go outside,
a young boy tries to catch the last leaf on a tree, thinking it will bring him luck.
ISBN-13: 978-0-8027-8924-2 • ISBN-10: 0-8027-8924-2 (hardcover)
ISBN-13: 978-0-8027-8925-9 • ISBN-10: 0-8027-8925-0 (reinforced)
[1. Luck—Fiction. 2. Leaves—Fiction. 3. Video games—Fiction.] I. Title
PZ7.O526Lu 2004   [E]—dc22   2003068868
_____

ISBN-13: 978-0-8027-9647-9 • ISBN-10: 0-8027-9647-8 (paperback)

The illustrations for this book were inked on layout paper with a Hunt nib and colored in PhotoShop.

Book design by Nicole Gastonguay

Visit Walker & Company's Web site at
www.bloomsburykids.com

Printed in China by South China Printing
Company, Dongguan City, Guangdong
10 9 8 7 6 5 4

All papers used by Walker & Company
are natural, recyclable products made from
wood grown in well-managed forests. The
manufacturing processes conform to the
environmental regulations of the country
of origin.

FOR NOAH AND CONNOR —K.O.